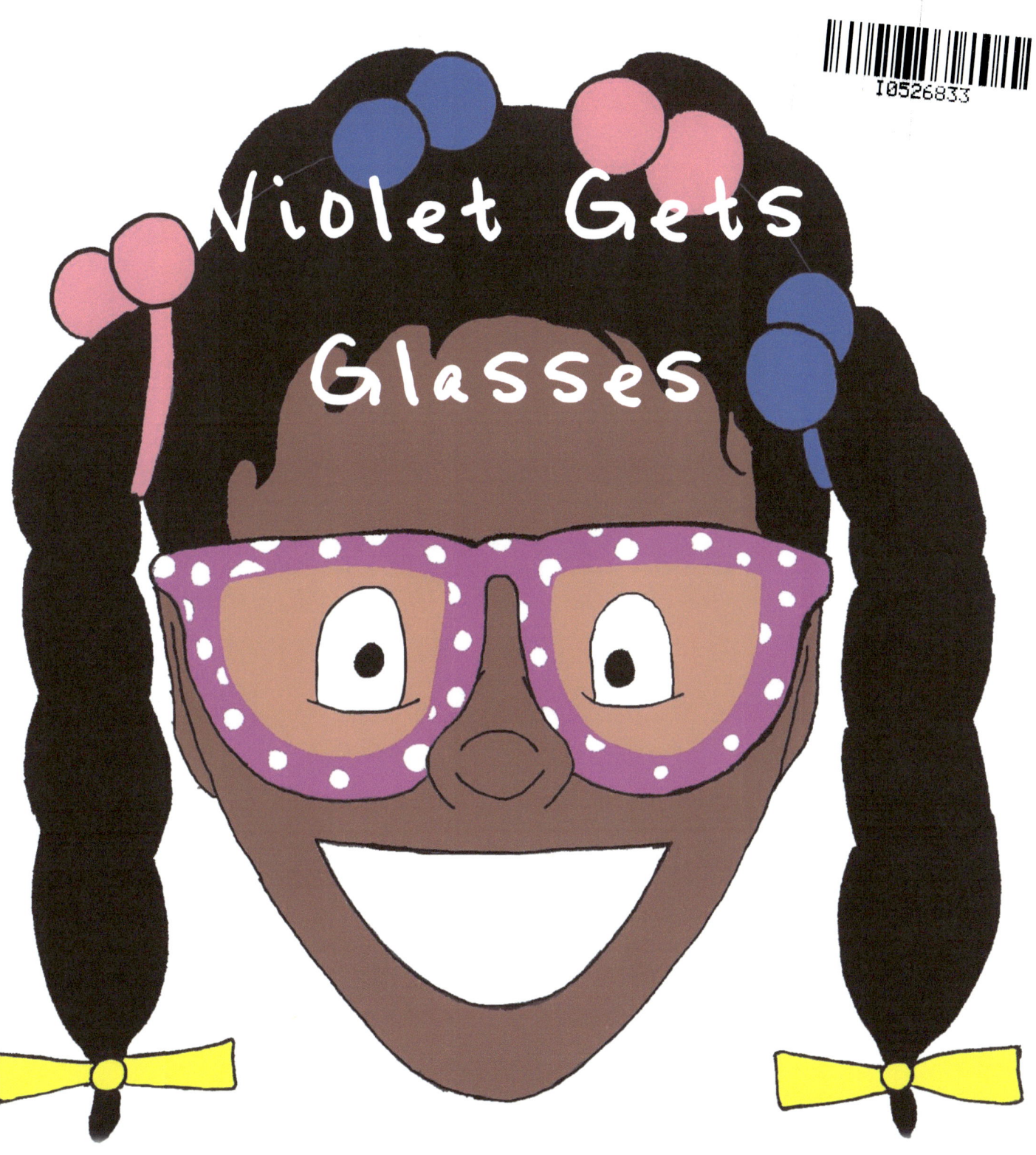

Violet Gets Glasses

ISBN: 9780578810768

Library of Congress Control Number: 2020924372

@violet_presents

This book belongs to:

_____

- - - - - - - - - - - - - - - -

_____

Everyone would always ask me if I were
mad or sad, and I did not know why.

I am happy! See!

Sometimes it was hard to find my shoes!

"Oh no, Violet! Your shoes are not the same!" said Mommy

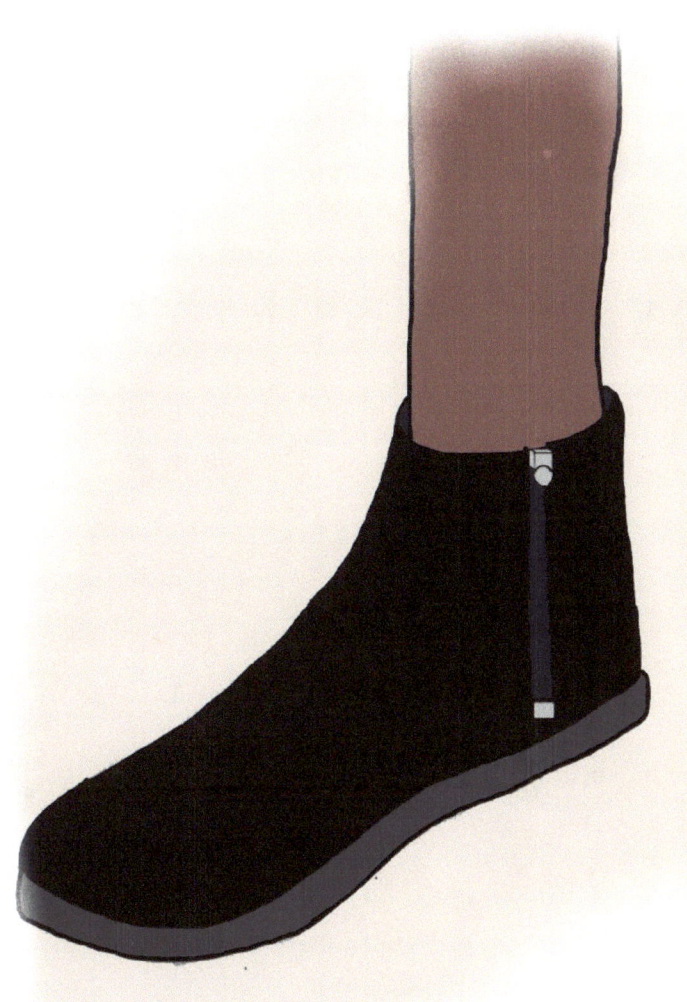

Mommy and I went for a walk and I thought I saw a puppy, but...

"Oh no, Violet! That is not a puppy. That is a cat!"

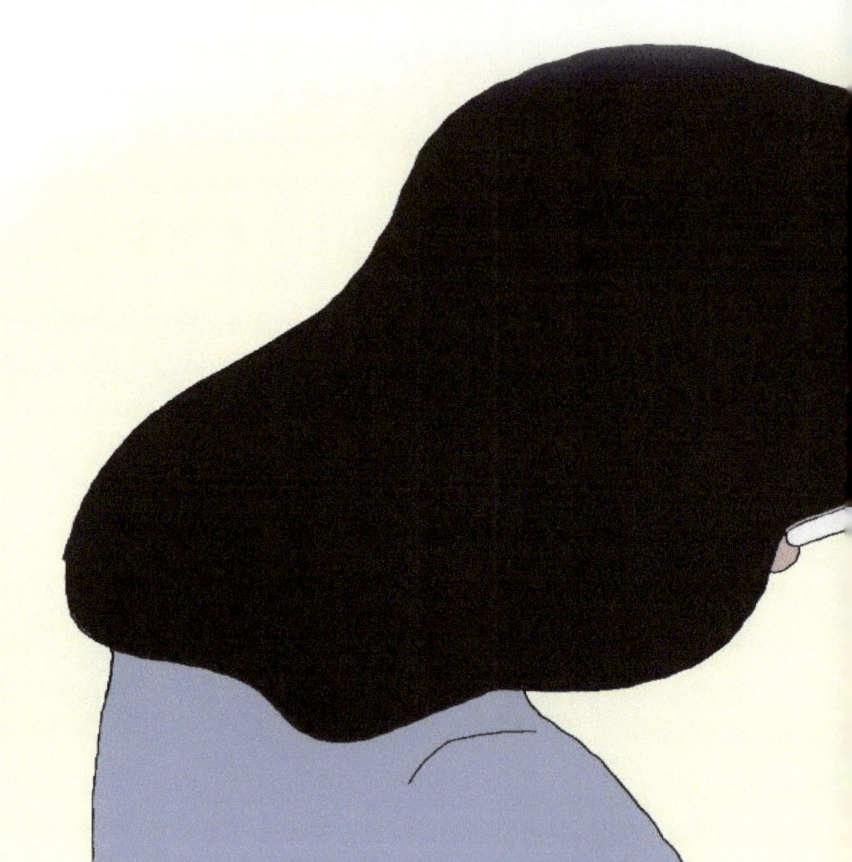

"I think it is time to go to the eye doctor to get your eyes examined for glasses"

said Mommy

"Can you cover your right eye and spot the purple circle?" asked the doctor

"Can you cover your left eye and spot the purple star?" asked the doctor

"Can you tell me on which side are you able to see the letter 'V' very clearly?" Asked the doctor

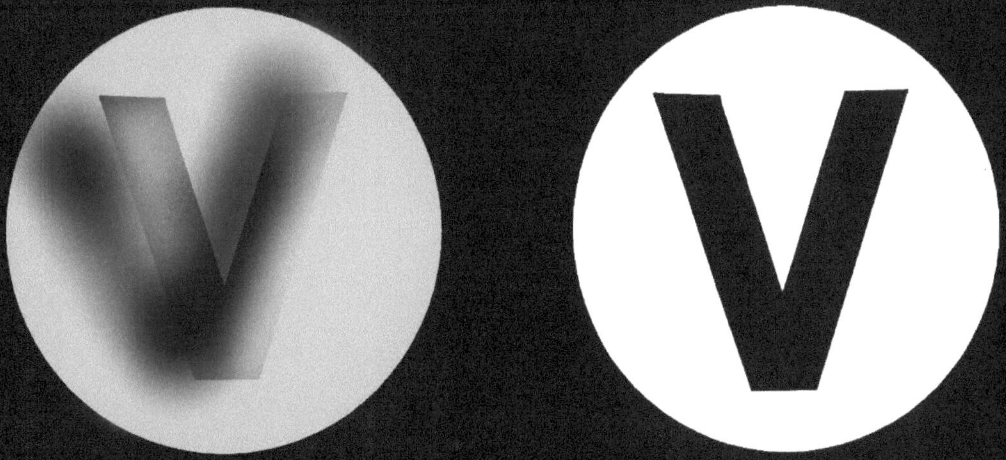
V
V

...and that is how I got my glasses!

Everything was so bright on the walk home!

"Look Mommy...
...a dog!"

...an airplane."

...a worm!"

"Mommy look! A cat
I can see!"

How to treat your glasses:

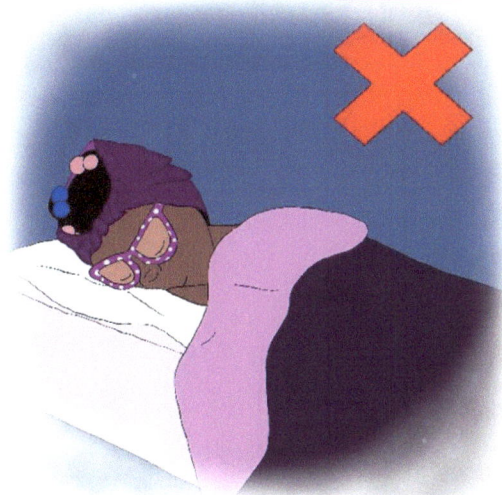

Do Not sleep in your glasses. This will bend and can break your glasses.

Do Not sit your glasses on the lenses. This can scratch the lenses.

When you take your glasses off, lay it on its side, or place it in its case.

Hello, I am TynishaSerena, and this photo is of me in kindergarten, in 1993.

I wrote this story for kids like me. For kids that, at a young age, benefit from wearing corrective eyewear.

www.ingramcontent.com/pod-product-compliance
Lightning Source LLC
Chambersburg PA
CBHW041009170626
46815CB00002B/232